First published in Great Britain in 1988
by Methuen Children's Books Ltd
11 New Fetter Lane, London EC4P 4EE
First published in Sweden in 1986
by Rabén & Sjögren Bokforlag, Stockholm
under the title *Skinn Skerping*
Text copyright © 1986 Astrid Lindgren
Illustrations copyright © 1986 Ilon Wikland
English text copyright © 1988 Yvonne Hooker
Printed in Italy

ISBN 0 416 07842 7

Astrid Lindgren and Ilon Wikland

The Ghost of Skinny Jack

Methuen Children's Books

Grandmothers are nice, especially ones who know how to tell ghost stories. We had a grandmother like that, my brother and I. She lived in a little red cottage on the edge of a long wooded hill, called the ridge. I'm not sure which was more exciting, the ridge or Grandma's ghost stories. But one thing was certain – it was fun to visit her.

One afternoon in November we set out on the long walk to Grandma's. We walked through meadows and fields and over pine-covered hills until we saw her cottage nestling in a hollow below the ridge. There she sat in her tiny kitchen – our nice grandma who could tell such exciting stories.

It wasn't long before we said, as usual, 'Grandma, tell us about Skinny Jack!'

And Grandma did just that. She always began in the same way.

'Hundreds of years ago, in the place where I was born, there lived a farmhand whose name was Skinny Jack.'

'But were you really alive then?' I asked her.

'Did I say I was? Of course not, you silly billy! But my grandmother could tell stories about him that made me afraid of the dark – foolish little thing that I was!'

'Had *your* grandmother seen Skinny Jack?' asked my brother.

'No, she hadn't seen him, but I think maybe *her* grandmother might have. Well, at least, she used to tell stories about him when my grandmother was little.'

'And now it's your turn, Grandma,' I said. 'Tell us the story.'

'Well,' said Grandma, 'Skinny Jack was a wild young man who was forever getting into mischief and doing crazy things, although he was the parson's farmhand and should have known better. Now if there was someone who Skinny Jack couldn't stand, it was the church organist. He could not get along with that man.'

'The organist was the one who played the hymns in church on Sundays,' said my brother to show Grandma that we were following the story.

'Yes,' said Grandma, 'and sometimes he played the church organ at night as well, because he had a key and could come and go as he pleased. And he loved to play music, both day and night. Now, one dark autumn night, Skinny Jack came up with an evil plan to scare the organist half to death.'

'What did he do?' asked my brother, although he knew as well as I did.

'That rogue, he dressed up like a ghost in a white sheet, and he put on a hideous mask that glowed in the dark. Then he sneaked into the church, where the poor organist was sitting so peacefully and playing so sweetly. Suddenly, there was the most dreadful bellowing and, up near the altar, stood the most horrible ghost you could ever imagine.

'The organist screamed and dashed for the door, as fast as his legs would carry him. But the ghost was after him, chasing him the whole length of the church. The organist ran for his life and, at the very last second, managed to get out of the door. Behind him came the ghost who didn't want to be left alone in the church either – he was afraid of ghosts! And then he got what was coming to him. Just as he made it through the church door, he felt someone grab him from behind. He was so terrified that his blood turned to ice. For who could be taking hold of him like that except another ghost or, worse still, God wanting to punish him for scaring the organist, and in church, of all places!'

'The next day was a Sunday and when the congregation arrived at the church, led by the parson and the organist, they found Skinny Jack lying cold and stiff right in front of the church door. But it wasn't a ghost, or God, who had grabbed him, it was the heavy church door that had slammed shut, catching the sheet and trapping Skinny Jack.'

'Was he dead?' I asked, even though I knew the answer.

'No, he wasn't dead,' said Grandma, 'but he wasn't alive either. Far from it. His blood had turned to ice and never flowed again. So Skinny Jack became a real ghost. That's what can happen if you scare someone in church! Neither the parson nor the congregation knew what to

do with Skinny Jack. They could hardly bury him, what with him not being really dead. So they simply propped him up, lifeless and stiff as he was, by the side of the road to church. And there he stayed.'

'For how long?' asked my brother, although he had heard the story so many times before.

'For a hundred years,' said Grandma. 'Long after both the parson and the organist were dead and buried, Skinny Jack was still standing there and haunting the place. People went out of their way to avoid him, they were so terrified of him.'

'But what about the parson's maid?' asked my brother, and I shuddered, because now the real story was about to begin.

'Well, a long time afterwards, a new minister came to live in the parsonage,' said Grandma, 'and he had a maid who wasn't afraid of anything – not even ghosts or devils.

'Now one autumn night there was a party at the parsonage. Lots of young people were there, and among them was one wild lad who wondered if it were really true that the parson's maid wasn't afraid of anything. "If you're so brave," he said, "then go up to the church and bring back Skinny Jack. I'll give you five crowns for a new dress if you do it." He was a rich fellow, with lots of money. Well, the maid laughed and said that such a dress would be easy to get.

'So she set out in the darkness towards the church. She picked up Skinny Jack, slung him on her back and carried him to the parsonage. She went right into the hall, where she dropped him with a thud onto the floor. Well, everyone shrieked with fright and the young man who had sent her out quickly gave her the five crowns. "Now you can carry him back," he told her. Ha! That's what he thought! "I only agreed to fetch him," said the maid. "You can carry him back yourself."

'But he didn't dare, and it cost him another five crowns to get the maid to do it. She wouldn't take less.

'So she went back out into the darkness again, that brave girl, with Skinny Jack on her back. She climbed the hill up to the church – and she wasn't afraid this time either. But, just when they got up to the church, Skinny Jack reached out and grabbed her!'

When Grandma said that, *our* blood turned to ice.

'Skinny Jack reached out and grabbed her' – they were the most awful words I'd ever heard!

'And he tightened his icy grip around her throat, didn't he?' asked my brother.

'That's just what he did,' said Grandma. 'He wanted the maid to carry him to the organist's grave, so he could beg for forgiveness for scaring him a hundred years before. The girl had to obey – you have to when a ghost has its icy fingers round your throat! So she carried Skinny Jack to the organist's grave and, with his horrible ghoulish voice, he begged the organist to forgive him.

'And then another ghost-like voice came up from the grave. It was the organist answering. "I forgive if God forgives," he said. And in that instant Skinny Jack collapsed and turned into a little pile of ashes. But the parson's maid was never really herself again,' said Grandma.

'I can just imagine,' said my brother.

Grandma's cottage had just one room and a kitchen, but upstairs there was a little attic. There were lots of interesting things up there, and when we visited her she usually found something to give us as a present. Now, after Grandma had finished telling us about Skinny Jack, she disappeared up into the attic. After a while she came down with an old guitar for my brother and a bundle of old illustrated magazines for me. How heavy my present was! But Grandma had a good idea – she put the bundle in a sack and tied it over my shoulder. Now it was easy to carry.

'You'd better hurry home before it gets dark,' said Grandma. So we thanked her, said goodbye and were out of the door before she could blink an eye.

'We can walk up on the ridge,' said my brother and, as usual, I did what he wanted. There was a narrow bumpy road at the foot of the ridge that sensible people used, and we should have taken it too, if we cared at all about getting home before it got too dark. But my brother started climbing up the ridge, plucking his guitar, and I scrambled up after him.

Up on the ridge there was a little path between the fir trees and the pines. It was like walking through a hall with pillars. Usually, I thought it was mysterious and grand, but just then, at twilight, it was nothing less than creepy. Besides, I was getting tired and the sack was very heavy. I just wished that I were home. I couldn't walk as fast as my brother and I started to lag behind. He was already far ahead of me, strumming the guitar to his heart's content. Finally he noticed I wasn't with him any longer.

'What's the matter?' he called. 'Is the sack too heavy for you?'

And then I shouted back – I still shudder when I think of it – I shouted, 'Yes, it's heavy. I'd rather carry Skinny Jack!'

How could I have blurted out something so awful! Why did I ever say such a thing? Ghosts come when they're called by name. I knew that! How could I have been so stupid!

And now the ghost of Skinny Jack was probably sneaking through the trees. Any minute now he would appear and say, in his horrible ghost voice, 'Aha! So you would like to carry me, would you? Well, you'll get your wish then!'

I tried screaming for my brother, but he didn't hear me, he was playing his guitar so loudly.

We were on our way down the other side of the ridge now. At the bottom was a hazelnut thicket that we had to go through to get to the road. My brother disappeared into it and I was scared to death. I was far behind him now and I felt more alone and abandoned than anyone else on earth. I couldn't go one step further. But I had to. I knew that Skinny Jack was hiding somewhere in the darkness. I had to catch up with my brother. He was in the hazelnut thicket. I could hear his guitar. I ran crying and gasping after him.

And that's when Skinny Jack grabbed me. Yes, he grabbed me! With his ghoulish hands he grabbed me from behind and held me fast. I screamed, but he didn't let go. I screamed until my blood turned to ice. I was finished, I knew that. Nothing could save me now.

But sometimes miracles do happen, for suddenly I heard my father's voice. Dad was standing there!

'What in the world are you doing here?' he asked.

'We've been to Grandma's,' said my brother. He was standing beside me as well now. 'What's wrong with you?' he asked. He put his hand on my neck and burst out laughing.

'You're stuck,' he said. 'Look here, there's a hazelnut branch caught in the strings of your sack.'

But I couldn't laugh even though Skinny Jack had disappeared as quickly as he had come. I could only cry. I cried while Dad helped me get loose, and while he untied the heavy sack. I cried when he carried me down to the road where the horse and wagon were waiting. But then I dried my tears and scrambled quickly up to the wagon seat. Everything was all right again – Skinny Jack had gone and I could rest my tired legs.

Oh, how lovely it was to ride all the way home! Luckily for me, Dad had been to the mill which wasn't far from Grandma's cottage. On his way home he had heard guitar music and loud screams coming from up on the ridge.

'And then I thought that must be the children,' he said.

I sat next to Dad as we headed for home and I held
tightly on to his arm, bouncing over the bumpy road in
the darkness. Behind me sat my brother. He had started
to play his guitar again, and now he was singing as well.

    '*In a deep and endless wood,*' he sang.

  That was one of our favourites, a sad song about a
poor little child who gets lost in a dark forest.

    '*In the wood a lonesome moan,*
     A child crying, all alone.'

Oh, it was so beautifully sad! But it had a happy ending
when the child came home. My brother plucked the
strings and sang the last verse.
'*Home, sweet home, and Father near,*
Home to everything that's dear.'
It was a happy ending for me, too. I wasn't all alone
any longer, crying in the wood among the pines and the
hazelnut thicket. Home, sweet home, and Father near
I had too – everything that's dear. And I wasn't caught
in Skinny Jack's clutches either!

But I could still remember the terror I'd felt, even when we were sitting at the kitchen table eating supper.

'Do you think that I'll ever really be myself again after all this?' I asked my brother.

'Probably,' he said. 'Pretty much so, anyway.'

Still I was a little worried.

'But what about the parson's maid?' I said. 'She was never really herself again. You know that!'

My brother laughed.

'You're not nearly as crazy as she was,' he said.